THE MISSION

AMMAD CHAUDHARY ASHRAF

Print information available on the last page

Rev. date: 01/18/2019

To order additional copies of this book, contact:
Xlibris
0800-056-3182
www.xlibrispublishing.co.uk
Orders@ Xlibrispublishing.co.uk

Once upon a time, there were four friends in a Jungle. They were called, Mr Rabbit (Hurricane), Mr Tortoise (Master), Mr Snake (Ring) and Mr Hedgehog (Spiky).

They were good friends. They would always meet up every day and stay together all day and play.

One day, as usual, they met up in the beautiful morning, but today was a bit different: someone was missing.

The Hurricane, the Master and the Ring were there but there was no sign of Spiky.

They were all wondering where Spiky had gone.

They all waited for Spiky for many hours but there was no sign of him.

When half of the day had gone and they were still waiting, they started to worry.

Then the Master [Mr Tortoise] said: "Hurricane, I think there is something wrong. Spiky usually turns up by this time; we should go and find out what the problem is; he might be in trouble."

"Yes, he usually turns up by this time, there must be something wrong," said Hurricane, thoughtfully.

"I think we should go and find out whereabouts he is before it gets dark," said Ring, anxiously.

So they all set off to find Spiky. They were looking for Spiky everywhere in the Jungle, up on the hills, in the streams and in the ditches, but there was no sign of Spiky.

Now it was getting dark. They were all very, very
anxious.

At one point, they thought they had lost their best
friend forever.

"What shall we do, Master? It's almost dark now
and we have gone all over the Jungle and there was
no sign of him," said Hurricane anxiously.

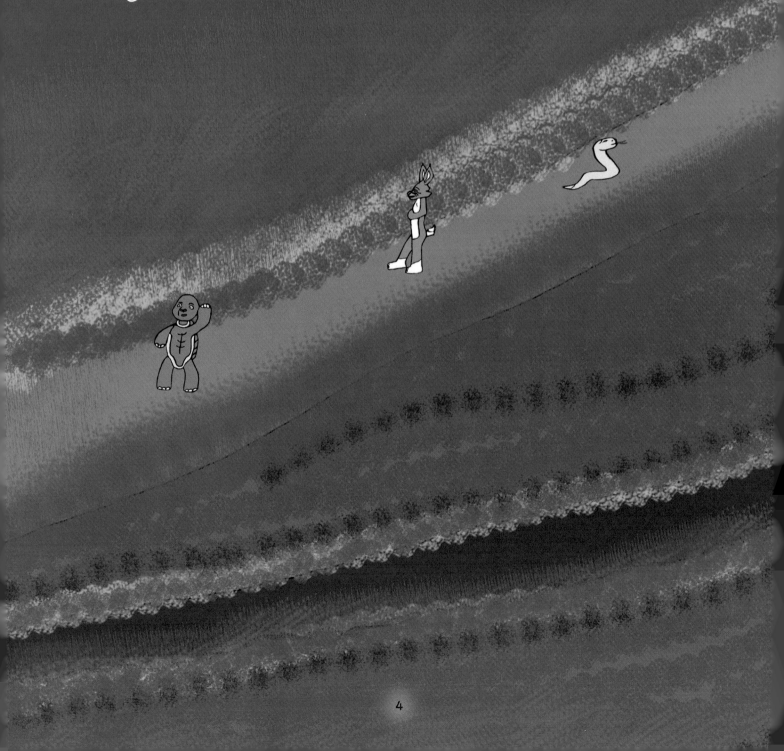

"I know we have been everywhere but we have no choice; we can't leave him like that, so we
will wait until it gets really dark, then everything will get very quiet and then we go all over
again and call him, because everything will be quiet and we may easily hear him,"
said the Master optimistically.

Hurricane and Ring agreed, so they sat down to wait. After a while it was really dark.
Then the Master said, "Let's go and find him; now hopefully we will find him, we will call
him and then go quiet to hear him, so we will go all over again in the Jungle.
Okay, guys?"

"Yes," said Hurricane and Ring.
They started walking in the Jungle again.

They all went again in the woodland to find Spiky.
It wasn't long before they heard some moaning coming from the bottom of a hill.

"Everyone stop and listen," said the Master.
They all stopped immediately, and started listening to the moaning sound.

"Spiky, Spiky, is that you?" said the Master curiously.

"Yes, Master, it's me, help me! Please help," said Spiky with pain in his voice.

"Don't worry, my dear friend, we are all here to help you: just hang on, we are coming," said Master emotionally. Then they all ran toward the sound.

In no time, they all reached the place where Spiky was.

When they saw Spiky, they were all shocked. It was an unbelievable scene for them.

What they saw was, Spiky, tangled up in metal wire. Spiky was badly stuck in the metal wire and he was bleeding badly.

They all quickly started to untangle him. After some struggle they successfully untangled him.

They took him to their home and treated his wounds and bandaged him up.

After a few days, when Spiky got well, his injuries were healed up.

Then they asked him what exactly happened to him.

''I was coming to meet you guys that morning and I was walking on the path; suddenly I felt something in my leg; when I turned around to find out what that was, I felt very sharp pain in my leg and I at once fell on the floor.

Then I realised that I was stuck in a sharp metal wire. I tried very hard to untangle myself from it but as I was struggling to untangle myself from it, I realised, I was becoming more tangled up in it.

I kept struggling to free myself for a while and then I got absolutely exhausted. I was bleeding from all over my body; I was in pain.

I had also been calling for help but it was unsuccessful. No one heard my voice, I presume, so no one came to help me.

Then that night, you guys found me and that's why I'm here today, with you, alive! I'm really grateful to you all.

Thank you very much, without your help I wouldn't be here now," Spiky sobbed.

"Don't worry, Spiky, you are fine now. We are all with you and we are also very grateful that we found you in time," said Ring while stroking Spiky's head.

"Yes, Spiky we have been very lucky to find you alive, and that was made possible by the Master's idea, that was to wait till it gets dark so then we would be able to hear your voice easily and we did, so we are grateful to the Master," said Hurricane.

Hurricane looked at the Master and said; "What are you thinking, Master? You are very quiet."

"Yes, Master, what is it? Why are you so quiet?" said Ring.

The Master came out of his deep thoughts, and said: "Yes, we are very lucky to find Spiky alive, no doubt about it, but if we had not been able to find him then think what would have happened; he could have died there, so we can't leave this matter like that: we have to do something about it." The Master was very emotional.

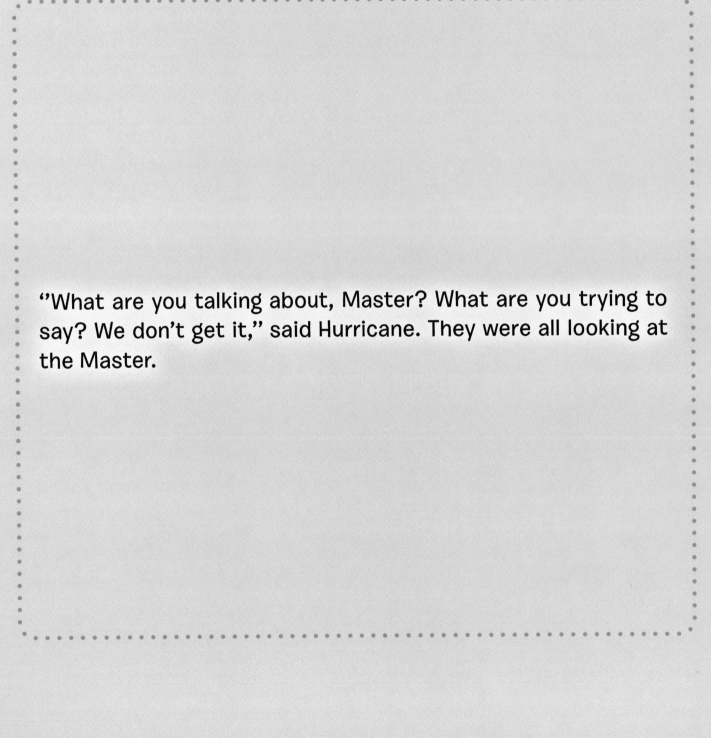

"What are you talking about, Master? What are you trying to say? We don't get it," said Hurricane. They were all looking at the Master.

"Well, guys, I'm thinking that we should clean up all the rubbish, whenever we find it. We must keep our paths clean and tidy at all times; that metal wire which entangled Spiky was thrown by a human being and there are lots of other things are all over the place, which were thrown by human beings; these things are very dangerous for everyone, even for the Jungle, for other humans and animals like us. I think this is a matter of life and death because it could be fatal to anyone, whether human or animals like us.

So from now on this should be our mission: to keep our home neat and tidy at all times. We will go to every corner of this Jungle and clean it. So everyone can be safe to go around."

"You are absolutely right! I agree with you and I'm with you in this mission: in fact we are all with you in this movement, aren't we guys?" said Hurricane excitedly.

"Yes, we are with you," said Ring and Spiky. "That's great, so guys, think that way from today, removing rubbish whether small or big from the paths.

"Think: it's like saving a life by cleaning the paths, and throwing the rubbish on the paths would be like killing someone; I think you wouldn't like to do the latter.

Are you agreed on that?" said the Master.

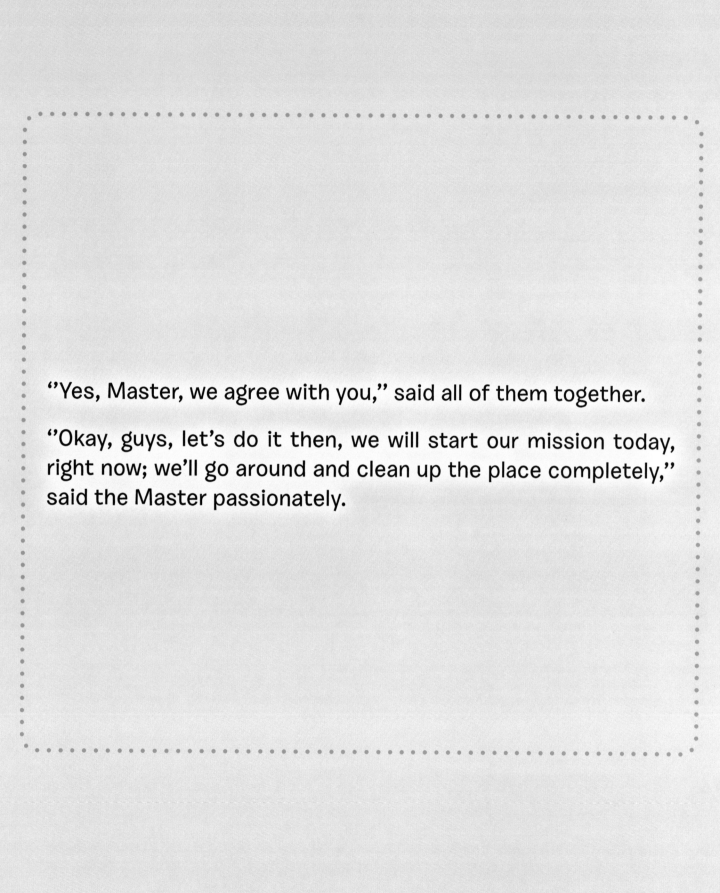

"Yes, Master, we agree with you," said all of them together.

"Okay, guys, let's do it then, we will start our mission today, right now; we'll go around and clean up the place completely," said the Master passionately.

Then they all got together and started their mission and cleaned up their home, the Jungle.

"So from now on, if you find any rubbish on a path, immediately clean it up."

THE END

Ammad Chaudhary is the author of two books;

'The Race'

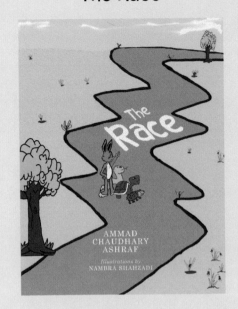

And

'The Mission'.

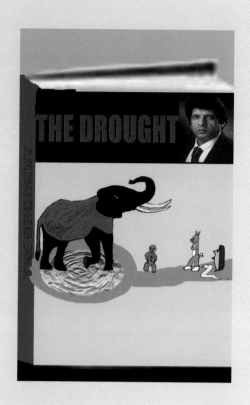

His upcoming book is titled, "THE DROUGHT".
Imagine that if one day you suddenly find that you are out of water!
Imagine that there is no water left at all!
Then what would happen?
You will find that out in the 'THE DROUGHT'.

Lightning Source UK Ltd.
Milton Keynes UK
UKIC022159030219
336550UK00005B/151